Stone Soup

by Katie Dale and Silvia Provantini

Once upon a time there lived a poor man who travelled many miles across the land. One day, he came to a village.

"Hello," he called to the villagers.

"I am hungry and have nowhere to stay. Will you help me?"

"You can stay with me," said a farmer.
"But our crops didn't grow this year,
so we don't have much food to share."
The others agreed. "Everyone is hungry,"
they said.

"You are very kind," said the traveller.
"I will cook you all some stone soup
to thank you for letting me stay."
"Stone soup?" the farmer frowned.
"What's that?"
"It's the best soup in the world,"
said the traveller. "I just need a cooking pot,
firewood, some water and a spoon."
The villagers hurried to fetch what
the traveller had asked for.

Soon, the fire was lit and the water was boiling. The traveller pulled a grey stone from his pocket and placed it carefully in the water.

The traveller tasted the soup. "Hmm," he said. "It would be better with some salt and a few vegetables. Oh well, never mind ..."

"I have some salt!" a woman cried.

"I've got a few turnips," said the farmer.

"I've got some tomatoes,"
added an old man.

They hurried off and fetched them.

"Thank you," said the traveller, and
he added everything to the pot.

The villagers gathered round. "When can we try the soup?" they asked hungrily. "It is nearly ready," said the traveller. "If only I had some meat scraps and garlic it would be the best stone soup I've ever made."

"I have some leftover lamb!" a man cried.

"I've got a little bit of chicken," said another.

"I've got some garlic," added another.

They hurried off to fetch them.

"Thank you, all," said the traveller.

The traveller added everything to the pot, and finally it was ready.

He spooned the soup into bowls and everyone began to eat.

"What is that wonderful smell?"

said a deep voice.

Everyone turned to see who had spoken.

There was the King in his golden chariot.

"It's stone soup, Your Majesty,"

said a farmer. "It's made from

a special stone. It's delicious!"

"I've never heard of stone soup,"

the King said. "I must try some."

The traveller passed the King a bowl of
stone soup.

"That is the best soup I have ever tasted!" the King cried. "I'll pay you three bags of gold for your special stone."

The traveller agreed and gave the King his stone.

The traveller took the King's gold and gave it all to the villagers.

"My stone was not special," the traveller told them.

16

"I just picked it up from the road.

It was your kindness that made the soup

so delicious, so the gold belongs to you."

The villagers gasped.

The King overheard the traveller's story.

"You mean I paid three bags of gold

for a normal stone?" the King cried.

The traveller nodded.

The King laughed. "You are a very kind and wise man, traveller," he smiled. "I'd like you to come and work for me at the palace!"

The traveller agreed and everybody cheered.

The traveller was given a happy home in the palace. He helped the King make wise laws to make the kingdom happier.

The villagers used their new gold to buy more seeds and animals for their farms.

From that day on, they all worked together, shared everything, and never went hungry again.

Story order

Look at these 5 pictures and captions.
Put the pictures in the right order
to retell the story.

1

The King tries the delicious stone soup.

2

The traveller arrives in the village.

3

The King hugs the traveller.

4

The traveller gives the gold away.

5

The traveller makes stone soup.

Independent Reading

This series is designed to provide an opportunity for your child to read on their own. These notes are written for you to help your child choose a book and to read it independently.

In school, your child's teacher will often be using reading books which have been banded to support the process of learning to read. Use the book band colour your child is reading in school to help you make a good choice. *Stone Soup* is a good choice for children reading at Purple Band in their classroom to read independently.

The aim of independent reading is to read this book with ease, so that your child enjoys the story and relates it to their own experiences.

About the book

When some villagers show a hungry traveller kindness, he offers to make them stone soup as thanks. The very special soup even gets the attention of the passing King!

Before reading

Help your child to learn how to make good choices by asking:

"Why did you choose this book? Why do you think you will enjoy it?" Look at the cover together and ask: "What do you think the story will be about?" Ask your child to think of what they already know about the story context. Then ask your child to read the title aloud. Ask: "What ingredients do you think are in stone soup?"

Remind your child that they can sound out the letters to make a word if they get stuck.

Decide together whether your child will read the story independently or read it aloud to you.

During reading

Remind your child of what they know and what they can do independently. If reading aloud, support your child if they hesitate or ask for help by telling the word. If reading to themselves, remind your child that they can come and ask for your help if stuck.

After reading

Support comprehension by asking your child to tell you about the story. Use the story order puzzle to encourage your child to retell the story in the right sequence, in their own words. The correct sequence can be found on the next page.

Help your child think about the messages in the book that go beyond the story and ask: "How does working together help make the stone soup taste so delicious?"

Give your child a chance to respond to the story: "What was your favourite part and why? Did you understand what the traveller was doing at first?"

Extending learning

Help your child think more about the inferences in the story by asking: "Why did you think the King gave the traveller a job?"

In the classroom, your child's teacher may be teaching how to use speech marks to show when characters are speaking. There are many examples in this book that you could look at with your child. Find these together and point out how the end punctuation (comma, full stop, question mark or exclamation mark) comes inside the speech mark. Ask the child to read some examples out loud, adding appropriate expression.

Franklin Watts
First published in Great Britain in 2020
by The Watts Publishing Group

Series Editors: Jackie Hamley, Melanie Palmer and Grace Glendinning
Series Advisors: Dr Sue Bodman and Glen Franklin
Series Designers: Peter Scoulding and Cathryn Gilbert

A CIP catalogue record for this book is
available from the British Library.

ISBN 978 1 4451 6938 5 (hbk)
ISBN 978 1 4451 6939 2 (pbk)
ISBN 978 1 4451 7298 9 (library ebook)

Printed in China

Franklin Watts
An imprint of
Hachette Children's Group
Part of The Watts Publishing Group
Carmelite House
50 Victoria Embankment
London EC4Y 0DZ

An Hachette UK Company
www.hachette.co.uk

www.reading-champion.co.uk

Answer to Story order: 2, 5, 1, 4, 3